Produced by The Creative Spark
San Clemente, California
Illustrated by Yakovetic Productions
Printed in the United States of America.
ISBN 1-56326-159-6

The Big Switch

Scales the dragon had worked all morning baking delicious cookies, pies, and other sweets for the Seashore Celebration, and now he was exhausted. "Being a dragon sure is hard sometimes," he said to Sebastian. The crab had smelled all the wonderful scents coming from Scales's oven and had stopped by to see how things were going. "I always have to do all the cooking," said Scales. "It must be nice to be a crab—*you* never have to do anything."

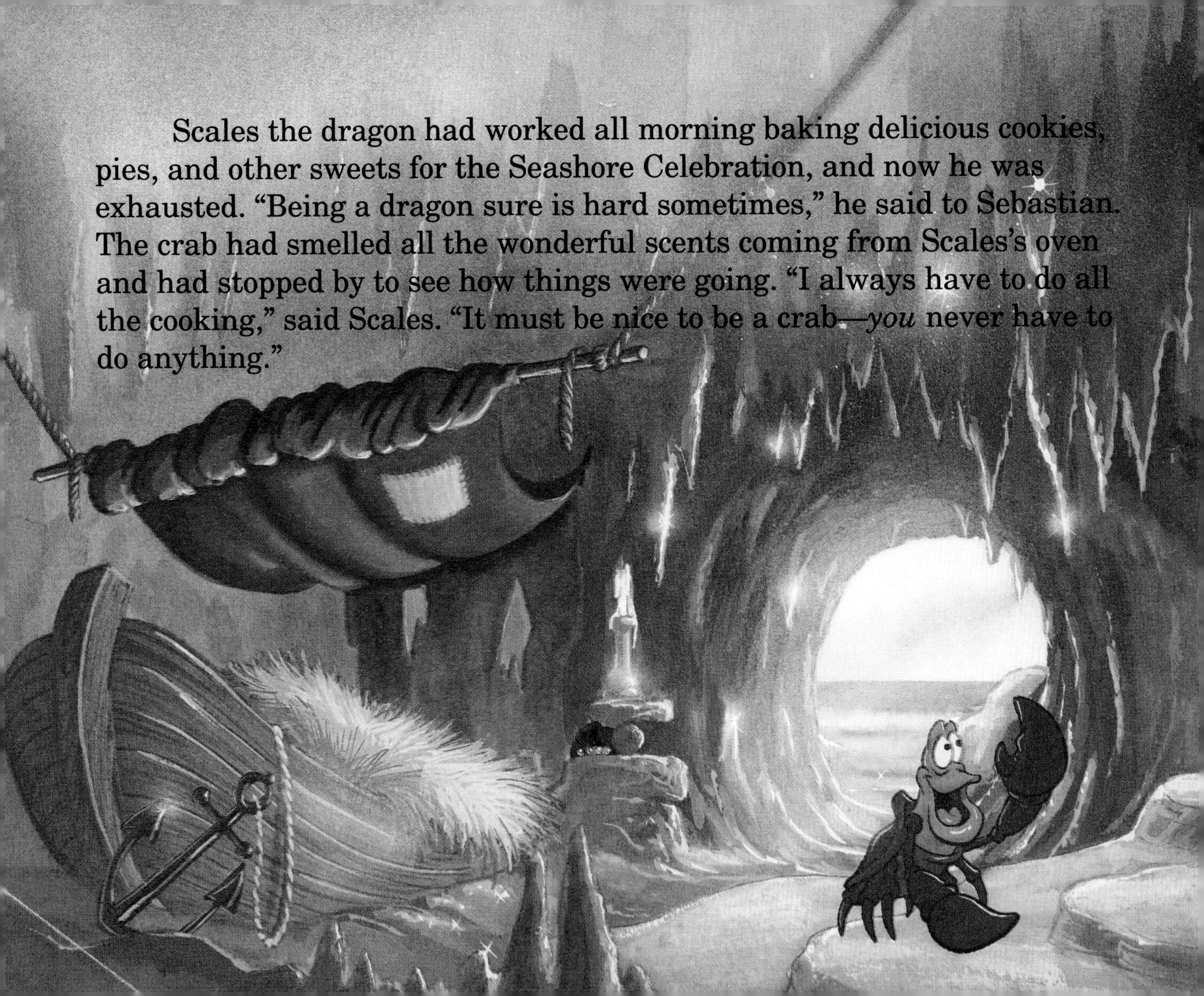

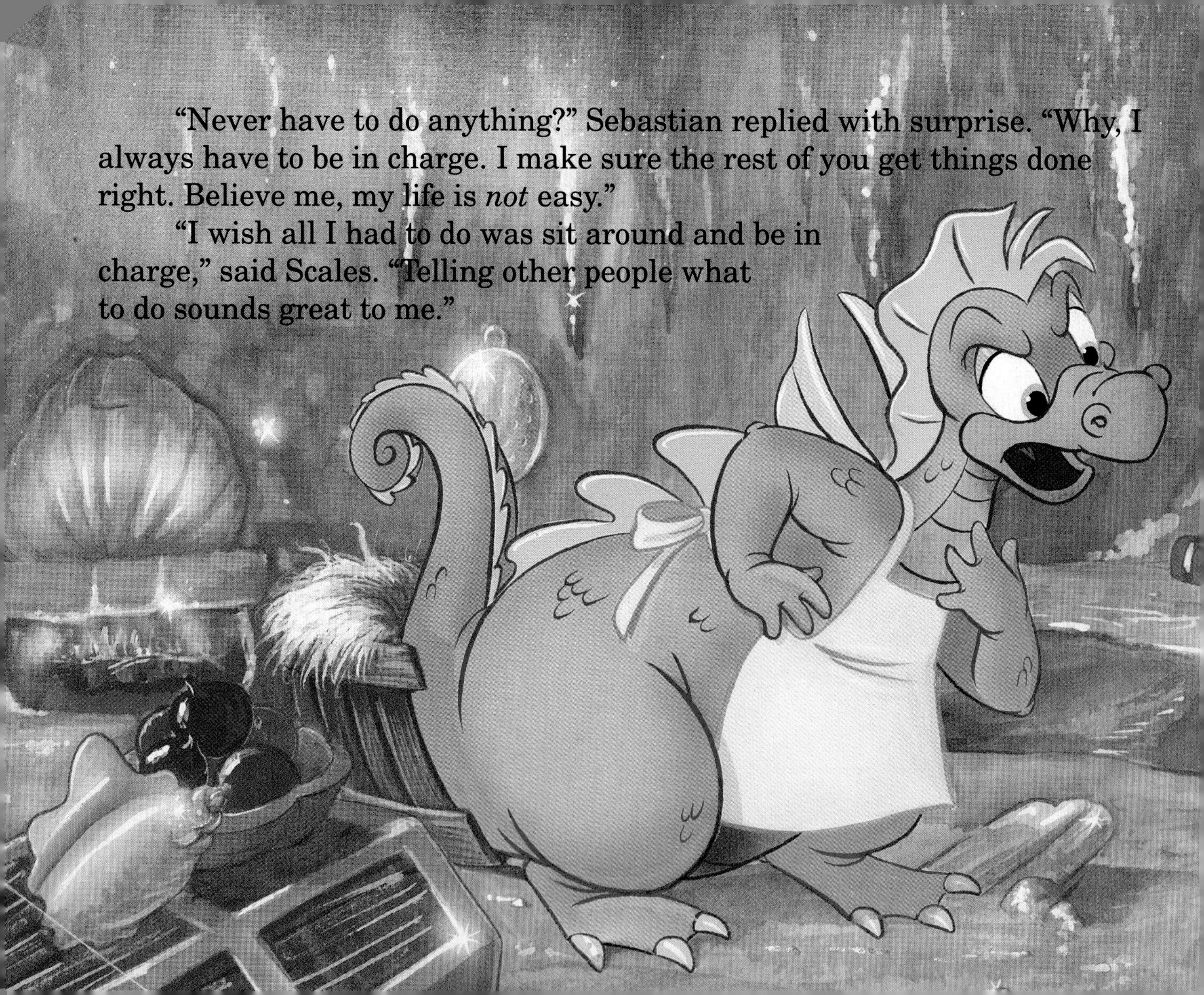

"Never have to do anything?" Sebastian replied with surprise. "Why, I always have to be in charge. I make sure the rest of you get things done right. Believe me, my life is *not* easy."

"I wish all I had to do was sit around and be in charge," said Scales. "Telling other people what to do sounds great to me."

“And I wish all I had to do was cook!” Sebastian said. “Making frosting and decorating cakes sound like *real* fun to me!”

“I’d like to see *you* try to cook!” Scales laughed.

“And I’d like to see *you* try to be in charge!” replied Sebastian.

And so the two friends decided to trade places for a day, to see who had the hardest job—the crab or the dragon.

As Scales took off his apron and left the cave, Sebastian found a recipe he liked in one of the cookbooks. He immediately started mixing up a big bowlful of seaberry batter. “This is going to be easy as pie,” he laughed, pouring in sugar and coconut milk. “You might even say it’s a ‘piece of cake’!”

Meanwhile Scales lay basking in the bright sunlight next to Sebastian's lovely tidepool garden. "Ahh," he sighed as the gentle ocean wind blew over him, "being Sebastian is a breeze!"

Just then, Ariel appeared at the edge of the tidepool. “Hi, Scales!” she called out. “What are you doing in Sebastian’s garden?”

“Sebastian and I are trading places today,” Scales explained. “He’s finding out how hard it is to be me, while I’m discovering what fun it is to be Sebastian.”

“Oh,” said Ariel, “then I guess that means you’re in charge of the decorations for the celebration.”

"That's right," Scales replied proudly.

"And that you'll be conducting the choir practice," Ariel continued.

"Yes, I guess so," said Scales.

"And making sure the beach is nice and clean," Ariel added.

"That's already taken care of," the dragon replied. "I told the crab committee to clean up the beach this morning."

"Just don't forget," said Ariel, "it's your responsibility to see that everything gets done on time."

Scales decided to stop by the beach and see how the crab committee was doing. But when he got there they were nowhere in sight, and the beach was a mess! Instead of neatly stacking the seashells the way Scales had asked them to, the crabs had scattered them all over the beach. *This is terrible!* Scales thought to himself. *There's no time to get them to do it again. I'll just have to do it myself.*

The midday sun grew hotter and hotter as Scales worked to clean up the beach. Just as the dragon sat down on a rock to rest, Flounder and Sandy swam by. "Hey, Scales!" they cried. "Come on! We don't want to be late for rehearsal!"

"Rehearsal?" Scales asked.

"Ariel told us you're pretending to be Sebastian today," Sandy said. "He's our conductor, and we can't start choir practice without the conductor. We're going to sing at the celebration, remember?"

Conducting the choir is sure to be more fun than cleaning this beach, Scales thought.

But he was wrong. At rehearsal, the clams wouldn't be quiet when Scales asked them to, and the seahorses were too busy seahorsing around to sing. Flounder and Sandy kept playing tag. No matter what Scales said or did, no one would listen to him!

After rehearsal, Scales went to check on the decorations for the celebration. He found Scuttle the seagull wrapped from beak to claw in a string of decorations. “These things are a little trickier than I thought,” the befuddled bird admitted. “Can you help me?”

“This is no fun at all!” Scales whined as he tried to untangle Scuttle. But Scales only ended up wrapping himself in the decorations, too. “I wish Sebastian and I had never traded places. Cooking is much easier than being in charge.”

Scales might think cooking was easy, but Sebastian didn't. The crab's first cake came out lumpy. The second one was all squishy inside. But his third cake looked as if it might turn out perfectly, after all. The minute Sebastian put it in the oven it started to rise just like a cake should.

It kept on rising, though, getting bigger and bigger until it pushed open the door. *Oh, no!* Sebastian thought. *What should I do?* The cake looked as if it would explode.

Which is exactly what it did!

"Being in charge is much easier than cooking," sighed the tiny crab when Ariel stopped by to see how things were going. "I wish Scales and I had never traded places!"

"Maybe you two should go back to being yourselves," the Little Mermaid suggested. "Being you is as hard for him as being *him* is for you."

"Do you really think so?" asked Sebastian.

"I know so," Ariel said as she wiped some cake off Sebastian's face.

Later that day, Scales and Sebastian met at the lagoon. "I'm sorry I said cooking was easy," Sebastian said suddenly.

"And I'm sorry I said you never did anything," said Scales."I guess I made a real mess of things. The decorations still aren't up, and the choir sounded terrible at rehearsal."

"And I ruined the food. There's cake and frosting all over your cave," Sebastian added. "Some friends we are—we've made a mess of the Seashore Celebration. Everybody knows you can't have a celebration without cakes and decorations and music."

But Scales had an idea. "Come on," he said, "there's still enough time for me to finish the cooking, if you fix the decorations and rehearse the choir!"

“I’m so happy to be cooking again!” Scales said as he merrily whipped up a batch of batter. Flounder and Sandy were happy, too, because they got to lick the bowl afterward.

"I'm so glad to be in charge again," Sebastian cried out gleefully as he waved his baton during choir practice.

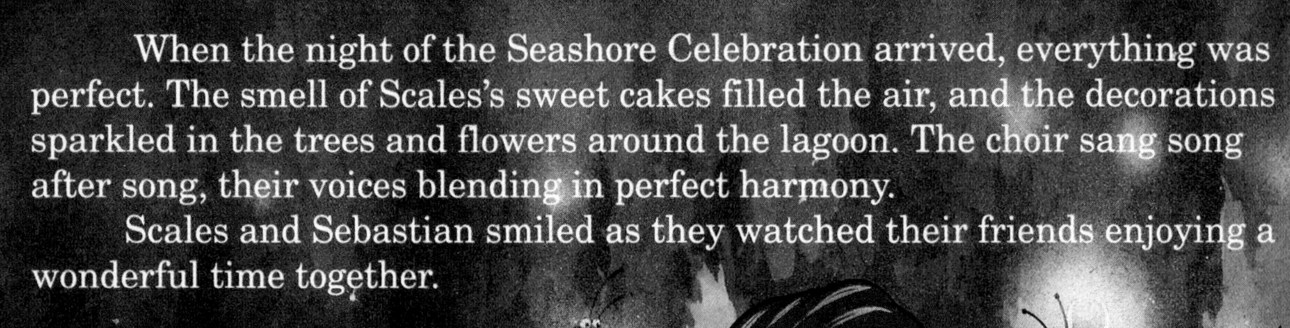

When the night of the Seashore Celebration arrived, everything was perfect. The smell of Scales's sweet cakes filled the air, and the decorations sparkled in the trees and flowers around the lagoon. The choir sang song after song, their voices blending in perfect harmony.

Scales and Sebastian smiled as they watched their friends enjoying a wonderful time together.

"You do a great job of being in charge," Scales said to Sebastian.

"Why, thank you, Scales," replied the crab, "but the only thing I want to be in charge of right now is eating some of your delicious cakes!"

"Would you like the recipe?" Scales asked.

"No, thank you!" Sebastian shouted and they both started to laugh.